This igloo book belongs to:

Elma♥ kandic♥

Published in 2016
by Igloo Books Ltd
Cottage Farm
Sywell
NN6 0BJ
www.igloobooks.com

GUA006 0316
2 4 6 8 10 9 7 5 3
ISBN: 978-1-78557-092-6

Printed and manufactured in China

Written by Jan Payne
Illustrated by Michael Terry

My Treasury of
AESOP'S FABLES

igloobooks

CONTENTS

The Boy
- Who -
Cried Wolf

One fine summer, a shepherd hired a young boy to protect his sheep from wolves. "Now remember," he told the boy on his first day, "you must shout loudly if you see a wolf near the sheep."

"What shall I shout?" asked the boy.

"Shout, WOLF! WOLF!" replied the shepherd. "I will come running and frighten the wolf away." The boy nodded and the shepherd left.

The boy was very excited to start his new job protecting the sheep from the hungry wolves. It seemed like very dangerous, important work. "I will watch them like a hawk," he said to himself, looking down the hillside at the sheep grazing below him.

The work was not as exciting as the boy had imagined. In fact, the first morning passed very slowly while the sheep ate grass. The sun grew hotter and hotter and the boy watched for wolves, but none came. At noon, feeling very bored, he ate a sandwich for lunch.

The afternoon seemed to pass even more slowly than the morning had. The dull sheep did nothing interesting, so to pass the time, the boy whistled a little tune and twiddled his thumbs. "I wish there was something fun to do," he thought to himself.

In the evening, the shepherd came and counted the sheep. "You've done well," he said to the boy. "I'll see you at the same time tomorrow for another day's work."

The next day, the same thing happened. The sheep ate their grass, the boy watched, and the sun grew hotter and hotter. Still, no wolf came. It was even more dull than the day before. The boy twiddled his thumbs some more and counted the sheep, but that only made him sleepy. He longed for some excitement. "If only a wolf would come," he thought.

When no wolf appeared on the third day, the boy was very fed up. "I'll pretend there's a wolf," he said to himself, "and see what happens." So, the boy called out in his loudest voice. "WOLF! WOLF! Come quickly! Come quickly!"

When the shepherd heard the call, he came racing up the hill, shouting and waving his arms in the air. "Where is the wolf?" he gasped, out of breath from running up the steep slope.

"He ran off when he heard you shouting," said the boy. "The sheep are safe, though," he added quickly. The shepherd praised him for his work.

"Well done, boy," he said. The boy knew he had lied, but he loved the praise and excitement. "Maybe this job isn't so bad," he thought to himself.

The next day, the boy couldn't resist doing the same thing again. Wanting the excitement of the day before, he cried, "WOLF! WOLF!"

This time, the shepherd brought other men with him. They raced up the hill, swinging sticks and waving their arms. The noise was so deafening that the boy had to put his fingers in his ears. Still, it was so much fun pretending to rescue the sheep from danger. "What happened this time?" the shepherd asked the boy after they had counted the sheep and found they were all safe.

"You frightened the wolf away again," the boy lied.

"Where exactly did you see the wolf?" the shepherd asked.

"Just there, next to the tree," said the boy. The shepherd went to look.

"I don't see any footprints," he said.

The boy didn't speak. He didn't look at the shepherd and his face went bright red.

The shepherd noticed the boy's embarrassment and spoke sharply to him.

"You are sure you did see a wolf?" he asked. "I shall be very annoyed if you have brought me all this way for no reason." The boy blushed again and nodded his head.

"I did see a wolf," he said. "I wouldn't lie to you."

For a while, the boy stopped pretending he had seen a wolf. He spent the next few days sitting in the sunshine, minding the sheep. It was so peaceful, he began to think that perhaps there weren't any wolves after all.

Then, late one afternoon, the boy saw a dark shape, half-hidden in the shadows of the trees. His heart raced. "It is a wolf," he whispered. He leaped to his feet. "WOLF!' he screamed. "HELP! WOLF!" From his house in the village, the shepherd heard the boy calling. "Surely the boy wouldn't dare try that trick again," he thought to himself, shaking his head.

When the shepherd didn't come to help, the boy panicked. He ran towards the village crying, "WOLF! WOLF!" at the top of his voice. The shepherd and the other men came out to meet him. When they saw how upset the boy was, they knew that this time he was telling the truth. Picking up their sticks, they ran towards the wolf and scared him away. "I'll never lie again," the boy declared.

The shepherd put his hand on the boy's shoulder. "I'm glad that you have learned a hard lesson," he told him. "If you lie all the time, then even when you tell the truth, no one will believe you." The boy nodded. He was so glad to have escaped the wolf that he never lied again.

*Even when liars tell the truth,
they may not be believed.*

The Town Mouse
- and the -
Country Mouse

There once were two mice, a rich town mouse and a poor country mouse. The mice were cousins but they hadn't seen each other in some time, so one day, Country Mouse invited his cousin to visit his home in the countryside. Town Mouse arrived on Country Mouse's doorstep in his finest clothes and shiny, new shoes.

"You look very nice," Country Mouse said when he met his cousin at the front door.

"Thank you," said Town Mouse. "I like to look my best for every occasion."

"I hope you brought other clothes, too," said Country Mouse. "The country is often colder and wetter than the town."

Town Mouse hadn't brought any other clothes and he soon began to wish he had.

"I don't wish to be rude," he shivered one morning, on a stroll through the woods, "but don't you find it rather cold and dirty here?"

"I'm used to it," said Country Mouse, who was sensibly dressed in a wool sweater and thick socks. "The air is fresh and pretty flowers grow in the dirt."

"In the town I have clean sidewalks to walk on," replied Town Mouse, dodging muddy puddles in his shiny shoes.

"If you have boots like mine, you don't need clean sidewalks," said Country Mouse, who was wearing bright green, rubber boots.

At dinner, when Town Mouse looked at his tiny plate of cheese rind and berries, he wrinkled his nose in dismay. "Forgive me, Cousin," he said, "but do you always eat such simple food? I am used to eating twice as much for dinner!"

"I don't need anything fancier," said Country Mouse. "If it's tasty, it's good enough for me. This is just enough to fill me up."

"You must come and stay with me and I will show you how much nicer it is to live in the town," replied Town Mouse.

"That is most kind of you," answered Country Mouse, politely. "I shall polish my rubber boots."

At last, Town Mouse's stay in the country came to an end. He hadn't enjoyed it very much, though he was much too polite to say so. When Country Mouse came to visit him, he couldn't wait to show him how much better the town was.

Arriving at Town Mouse's impressive house, Country Mouse looked up in amazement. The house was very tall and there were other tall houses on both sides of it. "Welcome to my home," Town Mouse said, rather grandly.

Inside the house, the floor was covered in thick carpet, so Country Mouse had to leave his rubber boots by the front door. It was so warm that he had to take off his scarf and thick socks. "This is a splendid house, Cousin," he said, looking at all the fine things.

Town Mouse served tea in the dining room. There was enough food to feed a thousand mice. Sandwiches and cakes, fruit and nuts, seeds and chocolate, but no bread and cheese!

"What a magnificent feast, Cousin," said Country Mouse, tying his napkin around his neck and preparing to dig in. "I have never seen so much food."

"Please try everything," said Town Mouse, "and have second helpings if you wish."

Country Mouse thought the food was so delicious he had second, third, *and* fourth helpings!

"I think I could get used to living in the town," he said, patting his wool sweater, which was feeling tight over his full stomach.

Just at that moment, a giant cat strolled casually into the room. "Have you started without me?" asked the cat. The two mice almost jumped out of their skin with fright. They dived straight into the bowl of nuts and scattered them all over the table. "Aren't you going to invite me to join you?" the cat asked, jumping onto a chair. "I'll sit at the head of the table."

This didn't appeal to the mice one bit. Quick as a flash, they climbed out of the bowl of nuts, ran down the leg of the table and escaped, in a flurry, under the door.

It was time for Country Mouse to leave. "You have everything a mouse could ever wish for," he said to Town Mouse, as they said goodbye, "but I miss my life in the country far too much." "I understand, dear cousin," said Town Mouse. They shook paws and waved goodbye to each other.

Back in his own home, Country Mouse settled down to the life he knew and missed. On chilly evenings, he sat by the fire and listened to the owls hooting outside. On warm, summer days, he played amongst the flowers in the garden and breathed in the sweet, fresh air. "This is the life for me," he said to himself. He remembered the giant cat in the dining room full of food and thought, "I prefer a simple life I can enjoy in peace."

Better a little in safety, than an abundance surrounded by danger.

The Ant
- and the -
Grasshopper

It was a lovely summer's day and the sun was shining. The grass was green, the corn was tall in the meadow, and the air hummed with the sound of bees. "I couldn't wish for a better life," said the grasshopper, swinging his long body on a hanging leaf.

He had just eaten a big breakfast and was as happy as could be. He was so content that he rubbed his wings against his big back legs to make a loud, chirping sound.

"I wish I could do that," called a small voice. The grasshopper looked around. On a nearby blade of grass was a tiny ant.

"Do what?" asked the grasshopper.

"Make that chirping sound," replied the ant. "Ants don't make sounds."

"So, what do you do when you're happy?" asked the grasshopper.

"I don't need to do anything," said the ant. "Just being busy makes me happy."

"Busy doing what, exactly?" the grasshopper asked, puzzled.

The ant was poking around here and there in the tall corn, searching for seeds. She couldn't even stay still for five seconds. "Busy making a home. Busy looking after my children. Busy collecting food for the winter," she answered. "I'm always busy!"

"Collecting food for winter!" exclaimed the grasshopper. "That's ages away."

"If we don't collect the food now, then we will be really hungry when winter eventually does come," said the ant.

"Poor Ant," said the grasshopper. "If you spend all summer working, you'll have no time to enjoy yourself. You should be more relaxed, like me." He stretched out in the sun, swinging gently on his leaf hammock.

"I must continue on, Grasshopper," said the ant. "Busy, busy, busy! It was nice talking to you."

The grasshopper watched as the ant picked up a grain of corn and carried it away. It was bigger than she was. "I'm glad I'm not an ant," he thought.

Summer passed and fall came. It was a bit colder and a bit wetter, but there was still enough food around if you knew where to look. Then, winter suddenly arrived and winter was different. It was very cold. Ponds and rivers froze over. The ground was hard like iron. The plants the grasshopper liked to eat stopped growing. There was no food to be found anywhere.

Now the grasshopper didn't feel at all happy. He no longer swung on his leafy hammock. He no longer rubbed his wings against his legs. He was too hungry and cold to play or do anything but cuddle up with a leaf for a blanket.

One day, the grasshopper saw the ant scurrying by. "Hello, Ant," said the grasshopper. "Remember me?"

"Of course," said the ant. "You're the happiest creature in the world." She looked closely at the grasshopper. "You don't look very happy today," she added.

"I'm not," said the grasshopper. "I'm miserable."

"Why is that?" asked the ant.

"Because I'm hungry," answered the grasshopper. "I'm cold and I'm weak. I can't jump anymore, or chirp. How about you?"

"Well, I'm not hungry," said the ant, "or weak. I have lots of delicious food stored up to eat." The grasshopper hung his head.

"I was lazy last summer," he said. "I don't have any food left."

"I'm sorry to hear that," said the ant.

The grasshopper looked at the ant with hungry eyes. "I can see that you are a very kind creature, Ant," he said humbly. "Please, will you help me, just this once?" "Of course I will," said the kind ant. "As long as you promise that next summer, you will change your ways."

So, all that winter, the ant shared her food with the grasshopper and when spring returned, he prepared to collect his own food. The grasshopper kept his promise to work hard and from then on, he was happy all year round.

Never put off until tomorrow what you can do today.

The Tortoise
- and the -
Hare

Once there was a hare and a tortoise who were good friends, even though they were very different. Tortoise was quiet and liked to do things slowly and carefully. Hare was the opposite. Hare did everything quickly and without thinking. He especially loved to boast about how fast he could run. "I can run faster than the wind!" he said to Tortoise. "You are slow. You just drag yourself along. I bet I could run circles around you."

Tortoise was fed up of Hare always bragging, so he decided it was time to teach him a lesson. "I may surprise you," Tortoise said, with a sly twinkle in his eye. "I always get where I need to go, in my own time. Why don't we have a race to prove it?" Hare laughed until he could no longer catch his breath.

"A race," he spluttered, "between a tortoise and a hare?"

"Yes," replied Tortoise. "Let's meet at the top of the hill tomorrow morning." The other animals gasped, but Hare just smiled.

"I can't wait," he said. He thought there was no way that the tortoise would ever beat him. He was a hare, after all!

The next morning, Hare and Tortoise met for the race. All their friends came along to watch and soon, a huge crowd had gathered. "Hare is the fastest animal of all. I know he will win," said Rabbit.

"I agree," said Field Mouse. "Tortoise is so slow, he'll never keep up with Hare."

Hare began to warm up. He ran up and down on the spot, touched his toes and did fifty push-ups. Tortoise just stretched out his little legs one at a time. When the time came, they both lined up at the start. "READY, GET SET, GO!" shouted Crow.

Hare shot off down the track like an arrow from a bow, running so fast it was almost as if he was flying. WHOOSH! Tortoise, however, started slowly and steadily, inching forward one step at a time. "Come on, Tortoise!" shouted his friends, but Tortoise didn't answer. He just kept his head down and lumbered happily on.

Soon, there was a huge gap between the tortoise and the hare. When Hare looked around, he could see Tortoise far behind and grinned to himself as he whizzed along. "This is so easy," Hare thought, smiling. "I'm sure I'll win this race."

A little way down the track, Hare saw a patch of dandelions in the grass. Tortoise could go all day without eating, but Hare ran so fast that it made him extra-hungry. He just couldn't resist the delicious dandelions! "I'll stop and eat," said Hare. "I'm so far in front, Tortoise will never catch up."

Hare ate and ate until he felt like he was going to burst. "I'm too full to run," he thought. "I'll just rest for a while. It will be ages before Tortoise gets here." Stretching out on the soft grass, he closed his eyes. He soon fell fast asleep and began to snore loudly.

A long way behind, Tortoise was still walking along happily. By the afternoon, he had reached the place where Hare was sleeping. "Oh, look! Hare found some tasty dandelions," he thought when he saw his snoring opponent. "I know he can't resist dandelions. He must have stopped for a snack and fallen asleep," chuckled Tortoise.

Unlike his fast friend, Tortoise wasn't hungry. He wasn't tired and he wasn't hot. So, while Hare slept the day away in the warm sunshine, Tortoise passed him by. He continued steadily on, getting closer and closer to the finish line without making any fuss at all.

When Hare woke up from his nap, he got quite a shock. It was nearly evening time and Tortoise was just a speck, far ahead in the distance. Tortoise had almost reached the finish line and it looked as though he was about to win the race!

Hare leaped to his feet and dashed after Tortoise. He ran faster than he had ever run in his life. He was so fast, his feet barely touched the ground and his ears flapped back in the wind. Flying overhead, the crow cheered him on. "Come on, Hare!" he cawed.

Hare got closer and closer to Tortoise, tying with him at the last moment.

"I'm going to win!" thought Hare eagerly. Hare stretched out his neck, but as they dashed over the finishing line together, he saw that Tortoise had beaten him by the length of his nose. All the animals cheered loudly.

Hare slumped to the ground, exhausted. "Well done, Tortoise. You were right all along," he gasped. "Sometimes it is better to take your time rather than rushing."

"Thank you," replied Tortoise, kindly. "Shall we have some dandelions to celebrate?"

"No, thanks!" said Hare, and they both laughed. From that day on, whenever he was tempted to brag, Hare remembered the day the tortoise had beaten him.

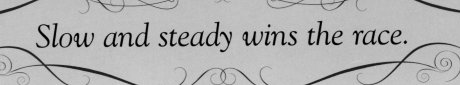

Slow and steady wins the race.

The Lion
- and the -
Mouse

One hot afternoon in the savannah, the lion was asleep. He snored so loudly that all of the animals in Africa could hear him. "What's that terrible noise?" asked the ostrich, lifting his head to look around.

"What's that awful racket?" asked the baby elephant, hiding behind his mother.

"What's that monstrous hullabaloo?" asked the rhino, drinking from the waterhole.

The rhino loved using big words.

The only animal who didn't hear anything was the lion himself. He slept so deeply that he didn't even feel two little mice running up and down his back, playing tag. As the snores of the lion grew louder and louder, the two little mice grew braver and braver. "You're it!" called one little mouse as he chased the other.

"No, you're it!" the other little mouse called back.

They chased each other along the lion's tail, down his legs, between his paws and in and out of his ears. When they could run no longer, they sat on the tip of his nose to catch their breath. "That was fun," said one, twitching his whiskers.

"Let's do it again," said the other, flicking his tail.

The twitching and the flicking woke the lion. He swiped at his nose with his paw. One little mouse dodged the blow and ran off. However, the other wasn't quick enough and he was knocked to the ground. The lion stared at the tiny creature, then opened his mouth to swallow it. The little mouse felt the lion's hot breath on his face. "Please don't eat me," he squeaked.

Surprised, the lion stopped what he was doing. "I'm hungry," he said.
"I'm so small, you won't even taste me," whispered the mouse.
"That's true," said the lion. He would need a much bigger meal to fill his large, rumbling belly.
"On the other hand," said the lion, reasonably, "I am the King of the Jungle. I'm not supposed to show any mercy."

"Dear King Lion," pleaded the mouse, "if you spare me, I promise you won't regret it."

"That's a big promise to make," said the lion, raising an eyebrow. He was curious about what the mouse might offer him.

"If you help me now," said the mouse, "one day, when you are in trouble, I will help you in return." The lion liked this idea.

"Ok, I'll let you go, just this once," he chuckled.

"Thank you, friend," said the little mouse. "I won't forget your kindness."

Though the lion had laughed at the little mouse, a few days later he did need his help. He was walking through the jungle, pushing the undergrowth to one side with his strong shoulders, when he stepped onto a trap. A net was hidden under a pile of leaves. The net closed around him and strung him up between two trees as the lion fought to get out. He arched his back and tore at the net with his claws and teeth, but the more he struggled, the tighter the net became. The lion roared in fury.

Far away, the mouse heard the lion's roar and stopped to listen. "My new friend is in trouble!" he cried. "I must keep my promise and help him." It was a long, difficult journey for a mouse. He ran all day and didn't stop until he reached his friend.

The lion was bound so tightly, he could not move. When he saw the mouse, he made a sad sound, deep in his throat. "Please help me, Mouse," he pleaded.

"Don't worry, dear Lion," said the mouse. "Be patient and I will soon set you free."

The mouse began to gnaw at the net that bound the lion. The net was made of thick, strong rope and even though the mouse could only chew a little at a time, his teeth were sharp. Slowly, each strand of rope began to fray and break.

Afraid and in pain, the lion could do nothing to help. At last, a hole in the net slowly grew bigger and bigger. Finally, the hole was big enough for the lion to move. Using his last remaining strength, the lion strained at the ropes. They snapped one by one and the lion fell to the ground with a THUD.

The lion lay there, weak and out of breath, waiting for his strength to return. The little mouse watched over him, not wanting to leave until he was sure the lion was going to be all right. After a while, the lion was strong enough to get up. He thanked the mouse over and over again. "You saved my life," said the King of the Jungle, full of gratitude.

"Just as you once saved mine," replied the mouse.

From that day on, the lion and the mouse were the best of friends and always remembered the importance of helping one another.

Never dismiss an offer of help, no matter how small it may seem.

The Dog
- and his -
Reflection

A hungry dog was eating his dinner. "I could eat that all over again," said the dog, licking his lips. He looked at his mistress with big, brown eyes. His mistress patted him on the head. "I'm sorry, hungry dog," she said, "but there will be no more dinner for you until later."

~The Dog and his Reflection~

The hungry dog licked her hand. He was sorry, too. He fancied a big, juicy bone right at that moment. "I'll go into the village," he said to himself, "and see if anyone has any scraps of food I can eat."

When he reached the village, the hungry dog headed straight for the butcher's store. He pressed his nose against the window and looked at all the meat on display. There was beef and lamb and pork and chicken. There were chops and ribs and succulent slices of pink ham. There were joints of meat so large the dog didn't think he could carry them, although he would have liked to have been able to try! Everything he saw made his mouth water more. "If only I could have just one of them," he drooled. "I don't think I would ever be hungry again."

Watching the hungry dog from inside the shop was the butcher. He was a kind man and when he saw the dog's face pressed against the window, he felt sorry for him. "I've never seen a hungrier-looking dog," he said to himself.

Behind him, on a marble slab, was a juicy bone. It still had a lot of meat on it. "That will make a nice meal for him," thought the butcher, so he carried the bone out of the store and held it out to the dog. The hungry dog looked longingly from the bone to the butcher. "It's yours," the butcher told him.

Hardly daring to believe his luck, the hungry dog took the bone in his mouth. Then, wagging his tail to say, "Thank you!" he ran off. The dog didn't stop until he came to a bridge that crossed over a small stream. "I'll rest here for a moment," he said to himself, and he looked over the bridge into the clear water running beneath.

What a shock he had. Below him, in the water, he could see another dog. This dog had a juicy bone clamped between his teeth, just like he did! "His bone looks bigger than mine," thought the hungry dog, enviously, and he opened his mouth to bark at the other dog.

As soon as the dog opened his mouth, his juicy bone fell from between his teeth and into the water. The bone made a great splash, creating ripples and waves in the stream. Suddenly, the other dog disappeared. The hungry dog realized he had just been looking at his own reflection.

He watched as the rushing water washed his precious bone downstream. Now, instead of two juicy bones, he had none. Because he had been so greedy, he had lost everything. Feeling very disappointed, the dog lay on the bridge with his head resting on his paws. "If only I had been satisfied with just one bone," he thought, sadly.

When the hungry dog arrived home, his mistress was waiting for him. "I've been looking for you everywhere," she said. "I have something for you." The dog's mistress held up a large, juicy bone. "I found this in the stream that runs through the bottom of the garden."

The hungry dog couldn't believe his eyes. It was his bone that the butcher had given him. The bone that he had so stupidly lost in the stream. Gently, he took the bone from his mistress and wagged his tail. As he finally settled down to eat his tasty treat, the dog vowed never to be greedy again.

Always be satisfied with what you have, or risk losing it.

The North Wind
- and the -
Sun

The North Wind looked down on the earth and was pleased with what he saw. He had been blowing all night and he could see the difference he had made to the land. Lines of tall poplar trees were bent over, their branches almost touching the ground and thousands of dandelion seeds were blowing like small white parachutes over the bare fields.

The North Wind was so pleased, he sang a little song.

"The North Wind doth blow and we shall have snow and what will poor Robin do then, poor thing? He'll sleep in a barn and keep himself warm and hide his head under his wing, poor thing."

In the same sky, the Sun also looked down on the earth and was pleased with what he saw. His warm rays had made the sunflowers turn their gold faces towards him. The bare trees of winter were green again and the little Robin, no longer cold, had come out of his hiding place and was hopping on the sunlit grass, looking for worms. "This is the world I like," said the Sun, smiling. "A world of light and happiness."

The North Wind and the Sun each thought they were stronger than the other.

"When I blow," said the North Wind, "the trees bow to my command. The seas rise up and flood the shore. Children hold on to lampposts to stop from being blown away. Everyone notices the North Wind!" The Sun disagreed.

"I have a far greater effect," he said. "I make things grow and flourish and feel better. The power of the Sun is stronger than anything."

"Let us have a contest, then," said the North Wind. "Let us see which of us can remove the coat of the man reading under that apple tree."

The Sun agreed. "You go first," he said. The man under the apple tree had no idea what was coming. He sat turning the pages of his book, enjoying the peace and quiet of a lovely, sunny day. Above, the North Wind puffed up his cheeks and blew as hard as he could.

The sky grew dark. The branches of the apple tree began to sway violently and all the apples fell to the ground. Pages were whipped out of the man's book and scattered in the wind. The man had to hang onto his hat and coat to stop them from being blown off. "I shall remove his coat by sheer force," the North Wind shouted, blowing even harder.

However hard the North Wind blew, he couldn't remove the man's coat and hat. "I shall try a different method," said the Sun.

The Sun filled the sky with a warm, golden light. The air became calm. The apple tree stood upright and the pages of the man's book settled on the ground. The man under the apple tree relaxed. He began to feel warm again. He took off his hat and unbuttoned his coat. "What a wonderful summer's day," the man said. "I no longer need such warm clothes," and he took off his coat and laid it on the grass. Then, he stretched out in the sun and went to sleep.

The Sun turned to the North Wind. "You can't always force people to do want you want," he said. "Sometimes it's better to persuade them."

"Perhaps my methods were a little harsh," admitted the North Wind.

"We are very different," the Sun said, "but we can still be good friends."

The North Wind and the Sun began to laugh together about their foolish contest and below them, the man under the tree picked up his things and went home. The North Wind blew a small cloud in the direction of the smiling Sun and a few raindrops fell to the ground. A rainbow spread across the sky and the North Wind and the Sun had made it together.

It is better to persuade others than to force them to do what you want.

The Rat
- and the -
Elephant

Ratty Rat loved being the center of attention. If people weren't talking about him, or listening to him, then he frightened them or made a nuisance of himself until they did. He liked to frighten children by stealing their toast at breakfast. He liked to annoy old men by pulling their moustaches when they were asleep. He liked to scare old ladies by jumping out of dark corners and shouting, "BOO!"

Ratty's mischief was known throughout the whole town and everyone was terrified of him and his tricks. Once, Ratty ran off with the teacher's chalk when she was writing on the blackboard. Another time, he sat on a lady's hat while she was singing in the church choir.

There was nothing Ratty Rat wouldn't do and nowhere he couldn't go. He could squeeze through the tiniest hole. He got into bedrooms and classrooms and playrooms. "I am the boss of this town," he often said. "I keep everyone on their toes!"

One morning, Ratty saw a crowd of people standing by the side of the road. They looked as though they were waiting for something. "What's going on?" Ratty asked them. The crowd ignored him. Ratty wasn't used to being ignored. "What could possibly be more interesting than me?" he said to the crowd of people in an annoyed voice.

A moment later, he had his answer. Down the street strolled a huge, grand-looking elephant. On the elephant's back sat the king wearing his finest red and purple robes and his jeweled crown. Sitting next to the king was a large, gray cat.

As the elephant passed by, the people waved and cheered. Ratty Rat was enraged. "What are you cheering at?" he asked, running from one person to another, biting at their shoes and trouser legs. "It's only a measly procession."
"Go away, rat," someone in the crowd said. "We want to cheer for the king and his elephant."
"The king and his elephant!" spluttered the rat. "What's so exciting about the king then? If you feel like cheering, I'll give you something to cheer about."

Ratty Rat began showing off. He leaped into the air and did the splits. He did six cartwheels, one after the other. He did a fabulous double somersault. "What do you think of that?" he panted, trying to catch his breath.

The crowd did not notice him. All they wanted to see was the elephant, the king, and the large, gray cat.

Ratty began to feel angry. "I'll make you notice me," he fumed, and he snatched a balloon from a little girl in the crowd. Holding onto the string of the balloon, he floated upwards into the air. "Look at me," he called from high above. The crowd didn't even look up.

Suddenly, Ratty burst the balloon and began to fall, down, down, down. He landed on top of a man's hat. Exhausted, he lay there waiting for someone to start clapping, but nobody did. "Hmmph," he sighed. Now he was really mad. "Can't you see?" he shouted, "I am more important than any elephant."

"You're not as big as the elephant, for starters," someone in the crowd said.

"You're not as strong, either," said someone else.

"You haven't got big ears and a trunk," said another.

"Big ears and a trunk?" shouted the rat. "I've got ears, a nose, two eyes, four legs, and a tail. I'm just as good as any elephant and I'm much more fun."

Then, Ratty stood up on his hind legs, flung his arms out, and did a little rodent dance. "What can that boring old elephant do that I can't?" he asked, triumphantly.

The Rat and the Elephant

Watching all of this from his seat next to the king, was the king's cat. "Bravo," drawled the cat, bringing his two front paws together to give a long, slow clap. Ratty Rat finished dancing and did an elaborate bow. The cat smiled a sly smile. Then, without any warning, he ran down the elephant's trunk, leaped onto Ratty, and pinned him to the ground.

"Oi!" squeaked the rat. "What do you think you're doing?"

"I'll tell you what I'm doing," said the cat in a smooth, silky voice. "I'm teaching you a lesson you should have learned a long time ago."

The crowd of people laughed to see the rat squirming beneath the cat's paw.

"Not quite so cocky now, are you?" they teased.

"I'm better than an elephant, any day," said the rat defiantly, wriggling and squirming to try and break free.

"I couldn't pin down an elephant," said the cat, trapping Ratty beneath him even harder. "An elephant is too big and too strong."

"That's right," said the town's people. "It is far better to be big and strong than to be small and a nuisance. I don't think we'll let that rat scare us ever again."

"So, rat," purred the cat. "If I set you free will you stop pestering the good people of this town?"

Ratty didn't have much of a choice. He certainly didn't want to spend the rest of his life at the mercy of a cat. "I suppose so," he said in a grumpy voice.

"Do you mean it?" asked the cat.

"Yes," spat Ratty. The cat lifted his paw and Ratty Rat slunk away.

"That's the last we'll see of him," shouted the crowd. They laughed and cheered as Ratty scurried down a drain, never to disturb the town again.

Never be fooled into thinking too highly of yourself.

The Fox
- and the -
Grapes

One day on a quiet farm, the time had come for the farmer to have his dinner. He had finished all of his work for the day, left his muddy boots by the farmhouse door, and gone inside to sit by a warm fire.

At this time of day, it was the fox's dinnertime, too. With the farmer out of the way, it was the perfect time for Fox to strike. So, he came out of his den, slipped under a fence, and crept into the farmyard. He sniffed the air and started looking for something to eat.

Fox was very clever. He knew all the good places to find food and how to escape if he got caught. He had grown so used to getting what he wanted that he was starting to become big-headed. "This will be easy," he thought.

Fox searched in all of his usual spots, scampering from place to place with his shiny, black nose high in the air. He looked for apples that had fallen in the orchard and vegetables piled up in the old wheelbarrow. That evening, however, Fox couldn't find a single morsel anywhere. "I won't give up," he thought. "I always get what I want."

Suddenly, Fox spotted a big bunch of juicy grapes hanging over the gate. "Mmmm," he thought with his mouth watering, "I love grapes. What a treat!"

Eagerly, he went to pick the grapes, but Fox soon found that his little paws couldn't reach far enough. The grapes were much too high. Fox got on his hind legs and stretched to his full height, but he still couldn't quite reach. He jumped up and tried to grab the grapes, but missed and fell on his face. He ran towards them very fast, then leaped into the air, but that didn't work either. "I will find a way," Fox vowed to himself, as he lay panting on the ground. "I'll reach those grapes if it's the last thing I do."

The Fox and the Grapes

For the next hour, Fox tried everything he could think of to reach the grapes. He leaped, he hopped, he bounced, and he somersaulted. He even found a pole propping up the clothesline and tried to pole-vault!

Finally, he tried to parachute over the grapes using an old umbrella, but a sudden breeze lifted him high in the air and dropped him into a cow pie. "Yuck!" he cried. Everything Fox tried ended in disaster and the grapes remained untouched.

Then, Fox remembered the old wheelbarrow by the vegetable patch and had a bright idea. "I'll stand in the wheelbarrow!" he cried. Fox pushed the wheelbarrow across the farmyard and licked his lips at the thought of the juicy grapes. The wheelbarrow was very old and its rusty metal wheels began to creak and squeal. *Ee-ee-ee*, they went, as Fox wheeled faster and faster. *Ee-ee-ee!*

The noise was so loud that the farmer heard it. He ran to the window and stuck his head out to see what was going on. When he saw the fox in the farmyard, he let out a mighty cry.

The fox was so startled, he dropped the wheelbarrow and ran away as fast as he could. Fox ran and ran, all the way back to his safe little foxhole, only stopping once to catch his breath.

Glancing back at the farm where the juicy grapes hung, his empty belly rumbled and grumbled with hunger. "It's just as well that I didn't reach those grapes in the end," foolish Fox convinced himself later that night. "I bet they would have tasted really sour anyway!"

It is easy to criticize what you can't have.

The Ant
- and the -
Dove

It was a hot summer day and Little Ant had been working hard in the sun. She was desperate for a nice, cool drink of water. She searched and searched for a pond or stream, but she couldn't find one anywhere.

The further Little Ant walked, the thirstier she became. "I hope I find something to drink soon," she thought. Then, she lifted her head and listened. "I can hear bubbling water!" she cried and with a new spring in her step, she hurried forward. It wasn't long before she came to a fast, flowing river.

Little Ant stopped on the bank and gazed joyfully at the water. "Now I can drink and drink and never be thirsty again," she said to herself. Little Ant was so excited, she scurried down the bank to the river's edge. In her haste, she slipped and fell, tumbling with a splash into the water. Desperately, she tried to turn herself over and scramble to the side, but the water was so fast and the current was so strong, she felt herself being washed downstream. "Help!" she called in her small voice. "Help, somebody, help!"

Overhead, a white dove was flying home. She had been decorating her nest and was carrying a large leaf in her beak. She heard the tiny cries for help and swooped down to see what the matter was. She was just in time to see Little Ant splashing in the water. "Hold on!" she cried. "I'll help you!"

Diving down, the dove scooped Little Ant onto the leaf and flew her to the riverbank. She tipped the water very carefully out of the leaf. Little Ant rolled out onto the dry ground, soaking wet and frightened. "Don't worry, Little Ant," cooed the dove in her soft voice. "You're safe now."

Little Ant shook the water out of her ears and smiled up at the white dove. "You saved my life," she said. "How can I ever thank you?"

"I don't need thanks," said the dove. "I'm just happy to be able to help."

"Kind Dove," said Little Ant. "I hope one day I will be able to do something for you in return." Parting ways, the dove flew up into the sunny sky and Little Ant ran happily all the way back home.

Little Ant was eager to repay the dove's kindness and one day, she had her chance. She was scurrying across a field when she overheard two bird catchers talking. One had a pair of binoculars and a bag full of birdseed and the other was carrying a net. "My wife has always wanted a pet dove," said the man with the birdseed, as he saw the white dove pecking away in the field. "We have a nice cage at home that it will feel right at home in."

"Quickly," the man with the net said, "throw the seed on the ground. Then, let's hide behind these bushes and when the dove comes to eat it, we'll catch it in the net."

Little Ant heard the men speaking and gasped. "They are talking about my friend, the white dove. I have to warn her," she thought, but it was too late. Dove saw the seeds scattered on the ground and flew down for a nice, tasty lunch.

She hopped around, looking this way and that, but the bird catchers were well hidden. Dove felt safe, so she began to peck away without a care. Before she knew it, the man with the net reached out and flung it over her. "Got you," he said, triumphantly. Dove cooed and beat her wings. "Help me," she called. "I'm trapped!"

When Little Ant saw Dove being trapped in the net, she knew she had to be brave.

"To the rescue!" she cried, running forward as though she was charging into battle.

Little Ant ran straight up to the foot of the man with his net over the dove. The man was wearing sandals and no socks. One of his big, hairy toes peeked out of the end, right in front of Little Ant's face. "Perfect!" she thought. Then, opening her mouth as wide as she could, she bit the man hard and fast on his toe.

"OW!" yelled the man with the net, hopping around on one foot. "OW! OW! OW!" It hurt so much that he dropped the net and Dove wiggled free.

"Thank you, Little Ant!" she called as she flew into the air. "Thank you!"

Brave Little Ant smiled and waved to Dove, then she scurried away as fast as she could go.

"You saved my life," the dove told the ant when she landed in the next field.

"Just as you once saved mine," replied Little Ant, finally happy to have repaid the kind dove.

The grateful heart will always find a
way to show its gratitude.

The Goose
- that Laid the -
Golden Eggs

There once was a farmer and his wife who owned five gray geese. The geese each laid one egg every day which the farmer and his wife would collect to sell at the market. One day at the market, the farmer and his wife saw a white goose for sale. "I have never seen a white goose before," the farmer said. "She must be special."

"Perhaps she will lay a lot of eggs," his wife replied. "Let's buy her!" So, the farmer and his wife bought the goose and took her home, checking every day to see if she had laid anything. For a whole week, nothing happened.

Then, one day, the farmer and his wife went to the barn again to see if the white goose had laid an egg. The goose was sitting on her nest and she looked very pretty with her soft white feathers and yellow beak. The farmer's wife put her hand in the nest and felt around.

"Oh!" she gasped.

"What is it?" asked her husband. The farmer's wife held out her hand. Clasped between her fingers was a beautiful, golden egg.

"It's very heavy," she said, carrying it to the door so they could look at it more closely. When she held it up, it shone in the sunlight.

"This egg is solid gold!" cried the farmer in excitement.

The farmer sold the golden egg and with the money he made from it, he bought an expensive new tractor. "This will make my job a lot easier," he told his wife.

The next day, the goose laid another golden egg. The farmer and his wife danced around with joy. "I shall buy some new clothes," said the farmer's wife, looking down at her old dress and apron.

From then on, the white goose laid a golden egg every day. The farmer and his wife called her the Golden Goose. "Now we can have everything we want," said the farmer. "We will be happy beyond our wildest dreams," replied his wife.

At first, the farmer and his wife were very happy. They bought each other presents and went on lavish holidays. Soon, however, they wanted more.

They built a house as big as a palace and filled it with the most expensive furniture they could find. Their cups, plates and dishes were made from the finest silver. The farmer invited everyone he knew to dine with him and his wife and sometimes their parties went on for days. They hired servants to run the house and farm, so the farmer and his wife didn't have to work. Soon, they both became greedy and lazy.

One day when they were having breakfast, the greedy farmer said to his greedy wife, "If we want to have everything, then one golden egg a day isn't going to be enough."

"I agree," said his wife as she thought of all the things she could have with more riches.

"We will need at least two golden eggs each day," said the farmer.

"What about three?" suggested his wife.

"Or four?" said the farmer.

They went to see the Golden Goose. "We want you to lay as many golden eggs a day as you can," the farmer told the goose.

"If you don't," said his wife, "we will take you back to the market."

The Golden Goose looked at the farmer and his wife with her bright little eyes. She didn't like what she saw: two greedy people who always wanted more. She ruffled her soft, white feathers and turned her back on them. "Make sure you obey us," said the farmer and his wife as they left.

The Golden Goose had no intention of obeying the greedy couple. "I shall go and live somewhere else, with nicer people," she said to herself. That night, when the farmer and his wife were in bed, the Golden Goose said goodbye to the five gray geese and she disappeared.

When the farmer and his wife realized the Golden Goose was missing, they searched everywhere. "Tell us where she's gone," they shouted angrily at the five gray geese. They all hung their heads. The geese didn't like being shouted at. "We'll take you all back to the market," said the farmer and his wife. The gray geese remained silent. They loved the Golden Goose and wouldn't give her secret away.

"If you hadn't been so greedy, this wouldn't have happened," shouted the wife to the farmer.

"You were greedy, too!" he shouted back. After a while, the farmer and his wife grew tired of shouting.

"Let us go back to doing things the way we used to," said the farmer. So, the farmer went back to plowing his fields and milking his cows. His wife went back to making jam and cakes and feeding the chickens and geese. Although they had lost their fortune, they were content with their lives once again.

"I am glad we are no longer greedy and lazy," the farmer's wife said one day. "I don't miss the Golden Goose at all."

"Neither do I," replied the farmer as they both realized that theirs was a simple life, but a happier one.

If you allow your greed to consume you,
you will lose your riches.

The Man, the Boy
- and the -
Donkey

There once lived a man and his son who needed to take their donkey to the market because they could not afford to keep him. To make sure the donkey sold for a good price, they did everything they could to make him look as handsome and rested as possible. They gave the donkey a nice, long bath. Then, they took him into the stable and brushed his coat until it shone.

Last of all, they gave the donkey a good meal of oats and hay and let him rest. "It's a long walk to the market," the father said, "so if he gets some rest, he won't be too tired for the long journey."

As they packed their bags and got ready to leave for the market, the son asked his father which of them would ride the donkey. "I think it is better if neither of us rides him," the father answered, "then the journey won't tire him out. It would be best if he could arrive at the market as fresh as a daisy."

So, the father led the donkey and the boy walked behind. The day was fine and sunny and they continued happily on their journey, all three of them enjoying the walk in the clean, fresh air.

They hadn't gone far when they saw a group of women hanging out their wet laundry in the sunshine. The women frowned when they saw the man, the boy and the donkey walking along the dusty road. "They look like they're heading to town. That's a long trip," said one woman.

"I agree," said another woman. "What sort of a father allows his son to walk when he could ride?" The man overheard the women speaking and felt bad. To please them, he quickly lifted up his little son and let him ride the donkey.

Further along the road, they met some old men digging up potatoes. "Where are you going?" asked one man, straightening his bent back.

"We're taking our donkey to the market," the father told him.

"Goodness, that's a long way to walk," said the old man.

"Yes, it is," said the father, who was beginning to feel tired himself.

The old man turned to the boy. "Show some respect for your father," he said. "You should let him ride the donkey. His legs are older than yours." Straight away, the son felt bad, so without a second thought, he jumped down from the donkey's back and helped his father up to ride instead.

As they got closer to the market, they met some workmen repairing the road.

"You look hot and tired, young man," one of the workmen said to the boy.

"I am," the boy answered. "We have traveled a long way and the day is warm."

"Why would you walk when you could easily fit on that donkey as well?" exclaimed another man. "That seems very foolish to me!"

So, to please the workmen, the father moved over and let his son ride on the donkey, too. The donkey huffed and puffed under the weight of them both.

The boy, the father, and the donkey had nearly reached the market, when next, they saw some children playing. The donkey was so tired from carrying the man and the boy, that he soon slowed down enough for the children to gather around and pet him. "The donkey looks tired," one of the children said.

"I expect he is," the father said, "we have come a very long way."

"If the donkey is tired, you should carry him," said the children. "You shouldn't make him carry you!"

So, finally, to please the children, the father and his son lifted the donkey onto their shoulders and carried him the rest of the way to the market. This made the last part of the journey extremely difficult. The donkey was heavy and the father and the boy were hot, tired, and thirsty. They looked longingly at the village pond, wishing they could stop for a drink.

As they continued on, people started to come out of their houses and stare. They pointed and giggled and laughed out loud when they saw a man and a boy carrying a donkey on their shoulders.

"What a ridiculous sight," an old man said, pointing at them with his stick.

"I have never seen anything like it!" chuckled another woman, holding her sides and shaking with laughter.

"I thought donkeys were supposed to do the carrying, not the other way around!" someone else shouted.

"They must be crazy," mumbled one grumpy grandma under her breath.

"...or just stupid!" yelled the crowd together.

With that, everyone watching collapsed into fits of laughter, with tears streaming down their faces. Hearing all this laughter made the donkey very angry.

"I'm fed up," the donkey thought to himself. "I've walked miles in the heat and dust. I've been sat on and carried and laughed at. I feel like a complete fool!" His temper rose and rose, until he could control it no more. In a fit of rage, the donkey jumped down and kicked up his heels. With that, the man, the boy, and the donkey fell into the village pond with a great, big splash!

The townspeople stood on the bank and laughed even harder at all three of them flailing around in the water. They had never seen such a funny sight as a man, a boy, and a donkey swimming together. The man and the boy weren't laughing, however. They couldn't see the funny side of it at all.

The man climbed out of the water first and gave a helping hand to his son. The two of them sat on the bank to dry off in the sunshine. "How could this happen," the boy asked, dripping with water, "when we have tried our hardest to please everyone?"

"That's the trouble," the father answered. "We have tried *too* hard. In trying to please everyone we met today, we have ended up pleasing none of them."

There was someone who didn't mind falling into the pond and that was the donkey. He was just happy to finally be able to rest!

If you try to please everyone, you will end by pleasing no one.

The Fox
- and the -
Stork

The white stork was new to the pond. She had just moved into a nest nearby and wanted to make some friends. When the stork flew around to meet the other birds, everybody liked her straight away because she was a very lovely bird. She was graceful and elegant, but also friendly and trusting. "We'll be your friends, Stork," said Flamingo and Heron. "After all, we are very alike so we are bound to have a lot in common."

"Thank you," said Stork. "That's very kind of you."

Listening to this conversation was a fox. He was a sly creature who was easily bored and loved to play tricks on his friends. "I would like to be Stork's friend," he thought, "then I can play tricks on her, too."

Rustling out of the bushes, he greeted the birds. "You are looking very charming this morning, Stork," he said, with a smile.

"Thank you, Fox," said Stork. "How nice of you to say so."

"I was wondering if you would care to have dinner with me?" Fox asked.

"That would be delightful," replied Stork. She was very pleased to be making friends.

Heron and Flamingo didn't trust Fox at all. They tried to tell their new friend, but Stork was very fair and wanted to give Fox a chance. When she arrived at Fox's den, she was thrilled by what she saw.

Fox had decorated the table with bunches of wild flowers and berries from the woods and there were two white bowls. In the middle, a candle burned with a cheerful yellow flame. "This is lovely, Fox," said Stork. She was flattered that the fox had tried so hard to please her.

"Heron and Flamingo must be wrong about Fox," thought Stork to herself, as Fox led her to the table and held out her chair for her. "He has such nice manners, he can't possibly be as mischievous as they say."

At that moment, Fox brought out a pot of hot, steaming broth and set it on the table between them. "Would you care for some soup?" he asked, whipping out a ladle and looking at Stork. The soup smelled so delicious, Stork couldn't wait to try it.
"I would very much like some soup," she replied.

Fox poured the soup into the two white bowls. "Please start," he said, politely.

Stork leaned forward to drink, but the white bowl was so shallow, her long beak hit the bottom with a CLACK. At the other end of the table, Fox grinned to himself.

"I'm so sorry," said the Stork and she tried again, but the same thing happened.

"Are you having trouble?" asked Fox with a sly twinkle in his eyes, as he leaned forward and lapped up the soup from his bowl with ease.

"It is impossible for me to drink from this bowl," said the embarrassed Stork.

"Then I shall have to drink yours as well," said Fox with a grin.

When Stork returned home, she realized that Fox had played a trick on her.

Poor Stork's empty stomach rumbled and grumbled. She was still hungry, having eaten barely any of the soup Fox had made. "Flamingo and Heron were right after all," she thought. "He's a very sneaky little fox. I shall have to teach him a lesson!"

So, that night, Stork thought up a trick of her own to play on Fox. The next time she saw him, she asked Fox if he would like to have dinner together, this time at her nest. Fox was very pleased. "She must have forgiven my little joke," he thought.

When Fox arrived for dinner at Stork's nest, he noticed that she had made just as great an effort as he had for her before. The table was set with a pretty cloth and two tall jugs full of tasty soup were waiting for them. The smell of the soup wafted under Fox's nose, making his mouth water. He was so hungry, he couldn't wait to eat. Leaning forward to lap up the delicious soup, he found that his wide snout wouldn't fit into the narrow jug.

Now it was the Stork's turn to smile. "Having trouble, Fox?" she asked, teasingly.

"That was a mean trick," spluttered Fox.

"It's only as mean as the trick you played on me," answered Stork. Although he felt ashamed, Fox had to agree that Stork was right. As she started to giggle, Stork said, "You must admit it was a funny trick."

Fox started to giggle too, and soon they were both laughing hysterically. With that, Stork got Fox a bowl that he could eat out of and said, "I wanted to teach you a lesson. If we are to be friends, then I have to be sure you won't play tricks on me anymore."

"From now on you will be able trust me," said Fox. "I promise." The pair enjoyed the rest of their dinner as good friends and spent many more evenings together without playing tricks on each other.

Always treat others as you wish to be treated yourself.

The Bear
- and the -
Travelers

There were once two friends who were traveling together to a far away village. They had walked for many days, enjoying the beautiful countryside and all the animals they had seen along the way. They had watched birds flying high in the sky and rabbits playing happily in the fields. As they finally drew near to the village, they saw that they would have to pass through some dark and frightening woods to get there.

"I hope we don't meet any scary animals," said the smaller man. "I'm terrified of wolves and bears."

"Don't worry," said his friend. "We'll be safe if we just stick together."

They followed a narrow, winding path into the woods, staying as close to one another as possible. Before long, they spotted a wooden sign, nailed to a tree. The sign read, "DANGER! BEWARE OF BEARS!" The two friends looked at each other, nervously. "We've come this far," said the taller man. "We can't turn back now."

The deeper into the woods the two men went, the darker it became. They followed the path, but it was narrow and sometimes disappeared altogether. The smaller man's mind began to play tricks on him. Every tree stump and bush looked like a bear!

Suddenly, out of the trees appeared a real bear walking towards them. The bear lifted its head and sniffed the air, then slowly rose up on its hind legs and turned its head from side to side. The bear could smell them!

The man in front wanted to turn and run, but he couldn't. He was too scared. His feet were glued to the ground. "What do we do?" he whispered.

"Climb a tree, quick!" his friend answered from behind.

"I can't climb very well wearing this backpack, can you help me take it off?" There was no reply. When the smaller man turned to look behind him, the other man wasn't there! He'd run off and left his friend to face the bear alone.

The remaining man had to think quickly. He knew that a bear would not attack a dead creature, so he fell to the ground and lay as still as he could.

The huge bear lowered its head and sniffed the man from head to toe. The man felt the bear's hot breath as it sniffed around his ears. The man didn't move a muscle and after a while, the bear lost interest and wandered off.

The man on the ground finally lifted his head and looked around. When he was certain that the bear had gone, he sat up.

Just then the other man returned. "Are you all right?" he asked his friend.

"I think so," answered the man on the ground.

"It looked like the bear was whispering in your ear!" the other man said.

"Yes," his friend pretended, "the bear was giving me some good advice. It told me never to trust anyone who deserts you in your hour of need."

It is misfortune which tests the sincerity of friendship.

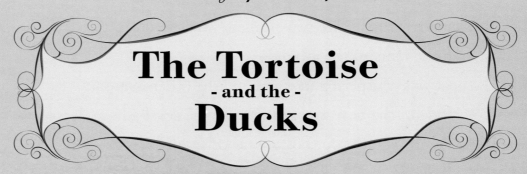

The Tortoise
- and the -
Ducks

Tortoise was feeling sorry for himself. "I don't like being a tortoise," he moaned. "It's so boring. I never have any fun. I have to stay indoors all the time and when I do go somewhere, I have to carry my house on my back." Tortoise drew his head into his shell and sulked. Then he popped it out again. "I know," he said in a happier voice, "I'll go for a swim. Swimming is the only way I can feel light and free." So he set off towards the pond.

Tortoise was walking along on his stumpy legs, when a rabbit ran past.

"Good morning, Tortoise," said the friendly rabbit. "It's a lovely day to go running."

"Good morning, Rabbit," replied Tortoise, keeping his head down. "I agree it is a lovely day, but I can't run. My legs are too short and my shell is too heavy."

"I'm sorry to hear that," said the rabbit. "I hope you can enjoy the day anyway." Then, he whizzed past Tortoise, over the hills and far away.

"Humph," groaned Tortoise.

A little further along, a squirrel raced past and ran up a tree. "Good morning, Tortoise," called the squirrel with a smile. "It's a lovely day for climbing trees."

"I agree, Squirrel," said Tortoise, grumpily. "It is a lovely day and I would love to be able to climb a tree, but my legs are way too short and my shell is way too heavy."

"I'm really very sorry to hear that, Tortoise," said the squirrel, apologetically.

He scurried away, up into the branches that Tortoise would never be able to reach.

Tortoise lumbered on until he came to the pond. Two ducks were flying in the sky, whizzing in circles high above him. "Hello, Tortoise," the ducks called, coming in to land on the smooth, blue water. "It's a lovely day for flying."

"Hello, ducks," answered Tortoise, miserably. "It is a lovely day for flying. It's also a lovely day for hopping and skipping and climbing trees and running marathons and going dancing, but I can't do any of those things."

"What can you do then?" asked the ducks.

"I'll just have to go for a swim," said Tortoise, dipping his toes in the water.

"Would you like to be able to fly?" the ducks asked, paddling alongside Tortoise.

"Of course I would," replied Tortoise, irritably.

"Well," they said, "if you hold onto the middle of this stick with your mouth, we'll grab each end and carry you up into the air."

Excited, Tortoise gripped the stick between his teeth and the ducks held both ends in their beaks. Flapping their wings and skipping across the water, they rose into the air, carrying the tortoise between them.

Flying high in the air was a wonderful feeling. Tortoise had never felt so happy.
He looked down on the tops of mountains, white with cold, sparkling snow. He saw
the fields of corn and flowers and the pretty, blue pond. He was finally having fun.

Just then, a crow flew past. He cried out in amazement to see a tortoise that
could fly. "You must be a very special tortoise," he said, squawking loudly.
Without thinking, Tortoise opened his mouth to speak. "I am special!" he bragged,
letting go of the stick.

Down fell Tortoise. Down past the mountains, down past the fields of flowers, and down past the blue pond. Down, down, down! When he could fall no further, he landed on his back in a field with his short legs waving in the air.

For a moment, Tortoise couldn't speak. All the breath had been knocked out of him. He wondered if he was still alive. Afraid for his safety, the ducks flew down to see if he was hurt. "Are you all right?" they cried, wrapping their wings around him.

Tortoise opened his eyes. He wiggled his toes. Then, he checked all the parts of his body to see if anything was hurt. Everything seemed to be working. He was completely fine! "My shell saved me," said Tortoise to the ducks.

The ducks gently turned him over onto his feet again. "Perhaps being a tortoise isn't such a bad thing after all," they told him. Tortoise stood unsteadily for a moment. "I think you're right," he said. "I will never complain again. From now on I will be happy just being me!"

Never disregard that which may prove to be the most valuable.

The Donkey
- and the -
Lapdog

There once was a farmer who had a donkey and a beautiful little lapdog. The lapdog lived in the house and shared all the things the farmer enjoyed. She even ate from the farmer's plate and she slept by the fire, in a basket lined with the softest fur. In the farmyard, the farmer would carry the lapdog under his arm so she wouldn't get her feet dirty in the mud. He loved the lapdog very much. "I don't know what I would do without you," he told her.

Life for the farmer's donkey was very different. The donkey worked hard. He spent his days pulling a cart loaded with hay, or corn, or potatoes and taking them wherever the farmer wanted them. Hour after hour, he dragged himself backwards and forwards across wet fields and along muddy lanes.

At night, when the farmer finally led the donkey into his stable, the farmer rubbed him down with a handful of straw and gave him some hay and oats to eat. "Sleep well," the farmer said in a kind voice to the donkey. "I have a lot of work for you to do tomorrow."

The donkey didn't have a bad life, but he was envious of the lapdog. He couldn't stop thinking about how different he and the lapdog's lives were. The donkey would watch as the farmer and the little dog ate together. The dog sat on the farmer's lap and he gave her the tastiest bits from his plate. Then he brushed her silky coat a hundred times with a soft hairbrush. "I wish I could have the things she has," the donkey thought when he went to sleep at the end of a long day. "I would love to be like her just for an hour," he said to himself.

One afternoon, the donkey was in the farmyard after a busy day. He glanced over at
the lit window of the farmhouse. The friendly glow made it look warm and cozy inside.
Moving closer, he could see the farmer sitting in his chair by the fire with the lapdog on
his knee. The farmer was petting the little dog and she looked as content as could be.
"I'd much rather be in there with them," thought the donkey.

Suddenly, a thought entered the donkey's head. "I know! I'll go in and join them," he decided. So, he snapped the rope that tethered him, kicked open the door, and burst into the farmhouse.

The farmer was surprised to see him. "You can't come in here," he said to the donkey, but it was too late. The donkey made a loud braying noise, rushed towards the farmer, and jumped up into his lap. Then he put his head on the farmer's shoulder and nibbled his ear. "Get off!" cried the farmer.

The donkey began to behave just like the little lapdog. He climbed onto the table and began to dance. All the plates and dishes fell off and crashed onto the hard stone floor. "Stop!" shouted the farmer. "Before you break everything."

"I'm having a wonderful time," laughed the donkey. "Look at what a wonderful lapdog I make," and he jumped off the table and kept dancing, not realizing that he was smashing all the plates and bumping into everything. In all the noise and confusion, the little lapdog cowered under the table.

The farmer began to get really angry. He chased the donkey around the room with a wooden broom, through the door and back to the stable, followed by the lapdog. Then he locked up the donkey quickly. "What am I going to do with you?" he sighed.

The donkey poked his head out of the stall and made a very sad face. When the little lapdog saw how upset the donkey was at being chased away, she said to the farmer, "Don't be unkind to the donkey. He only wanted you to love him as much as you love me."

Then the farmer felt sorry for the donkey. "I *do* love you, Donkey," he said. "I love you very much. I couldn't possibly manage without you. You are just as important to me as any other creature."

The donkey neighed happily and nuzzled the farmer. The farmer laughed, forgiving the donkey for clowning around. From that day on, the donkey was happy just being who he was and he never tried to be like anyone else, ever again.

*Happiness is found in being content
with who you are.*

The Peacock
- and the -
Crane

Once, there was a peacock who was extremely beautiful. However, his beauty had made him so vain that he spent every day admiring his reflection in the lake. The peacock would strut backwards and forwards with his tail spread out like a huge fan around him. He marveled at the beautiful blue of his elegant, long neck and the greens and golds of his magnificent tail.

The more he looked at himself, the more the peacock simply couldn't believe how handsome he was. He thought that he must be the most noble and majestic of all the birds. "I am surely the envy of every creature in the land," he said to himself.

One day, while he was admiring himself in the lake as usual, the peacock met a crane. The crane was a large and handsome bird, but he had plain feathers and strong wings for flying great distances in the cold weather. He was pale gray and white with black tips on his wings and was certainly not as dazzling as the peacock. "Good morning, Peacock," said Crane. "How are you this fine day?"

"I am very well, as you can see, Crane," said Peacock as he paraded up and down. His tail was fanned out as wide as it would go, so that Crane could admire it properly.

The crane was impressed. "Your tail is one of the most beautiful sights I have ever seen," he said, generously. "You must be immensely proud."

"I am, indeed," said Peacock, grandly. "Every day I give thanks that I am the most handsome bird alive. Look how my feathers shine in the sun. They are decorated with every color of the rainbow. In fact, I think my tail probably has even more colors than the rainbow."

The peacock turned slowly in front of the crane, his tail fluttering and shimmering.

The crane nodded politely in agreement. The peacock's beauty was truly a sight to behold.
Peacock continued boasting. "I am the jewel in the world's crown," he went on. "I am dressed
in the robes of royalty. I might as well be King of the Birds!"

The crane paused before replying. "What you say is true," he said. "I don't know anyone who
would disagree that your feathers are the finest in the world."
The peacock gloated at the crane's words and replied rudely, "It must be hard for you, poor
Crane, to stand this close to me, when you are so plain and dull."

"I may have plain feathers while you have the robes of a king," said the crane to the peacock, "but my life is far richer. While you see beauty only in yourself, I see the beauty of the whole world around me."

The peacock looked at the crane in disbelief, shocked that anyone could question his superiority. "I do things you can only dream of," continued the crane. "By day, I travel for miles and miles to new lands, where there are birds just as fabulously feathered as you are and at night, I fly so high I can almost touch the stars."

"I can fly a bit, too," said the peacock, blushing with embarrassment.

"Perhaps you can," replied Crane, "but can you fly over mountains and oceans? Can you fly high above the clouds and warm your wings in the rays of the sun?"

The peacock was silent while the crane continued to boast, "Just because I am not as beautiful as you, does not make me any less interesting than you."

At last, Peacock had to agree with Crane's wise words. With that, Crane began to flap his strong wings and took off over the lake. Peacock could only stand and watch while the crane flew off into the morning sun for another exciting adventure.

*It is better to have substance and value,
than simply to be beautiful.*

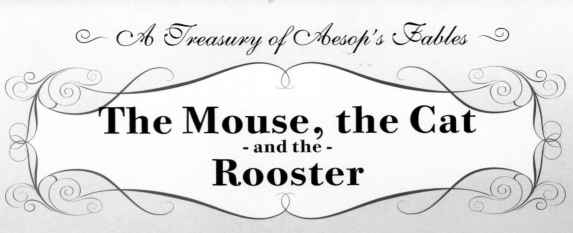

The Mouse, the Cat
- and the -
Rooster

A little mouse was in the farmyard looking for some food for him and his mother to eat for dinner. It was the first time he had been out on his own and the farmyard looked enormous. "I don't like this place," squeaked the mouse, looking around in fear. "I must find some food quickly and get back home." The little mouse didn't know where to start looking. He scurried around, peering and poking under this and that, but all he found was a horrible, smelly cow pie. The little mouse held his nose. "Yuck! I don't think anyone could eat that." he said.

Suddenly, there was a loud, piercing squawk and a big, bold rooster strutted into the yard.
The little mouse had never seen a rooster, so he stared wide-eyed at the creature in terror.
It was a magnificent, but strange-looking bird. It had glossy feathers of all different colors, a
scrawny neck and a head that bobbed up and down when it moved. On its head was a bright,
red crest. Its beak was curved and fierce-looking. "Cock-a-doodle-do!" cried the rooster,
strutting about the farmyard. "Cock-a-doodle-do!" The little mouse dived under a pile of hay.
"It's a monster who wants to eat me," he whimpered, shaking with fear.

The rooster saw the frightened mouse under the hay. "There's no need to be scared, little mouse," he said. "I'm not going to hurt you. Let me introduce myself."

The little mouse said nothing. His teeth were chattering with fright. He didn't like the look, or the sound, of this strange creature and he certainly didn't want to be introduced to him. He stayed quiet under the hay and listened to the monster scratching at the ground with his claws. The sound was horribly loud to the mouse's ears.

As soon as the rooster's back was turned, the mouse ran away as fast as his little legs would carry him.

The mouse ran out to the farmyard and straight into the barn next door. He had never been there before either. "Where am I?" he said out loud.

The barn was huge and very gloomy. It had a high roof with great big wooden beams running across it from left to right. Bales of hay were stacked up, one on top of another. On one of the hay bales sat a pretty creature with soft, shiny fur and eyes that looked as though they were made of green glass. She smiled when she saw the little mouse and hopped down from the hay bales to come closer to greet him.

137

It was a cat. "Are you lost, little mouse?" asked the cat. Her tail twitched and she started to purr. It was a lovely, warm sound, so much nicer than the harsh crowing of the rooster. The mouse was charmed by it. "I think I am lost," he admitted.

"Well, I'm sure I can help you find your way," purred the cat, silkily, "but first, tell me, are you all by yourself?" The little mouse felt he could trust the cat. Her voice was so soft and she seemed so friendly.

"Yes, I am," he said boldly, "I am looking for food for my mother."

"Your mother!" replied the cat in surprise. "So there are two of you? Well, let's find where you live and we can take some food to her together!"

"That's very kind of you," replied the little mouse. "My mother will be pleased to see you."

"I will be very pleased to see *her*," said the cat, her voice growing silkier by the minute. "Perhaps if you squeak loudly enough, she will hear you and answer back. Then we will know which direction to take."

"That's a fantastic idea," said the little mouse and he puffed up his chest to give his best squeak ever. SQUEAK!

Just then, the rooster strolled into the barn. "What's going on in here?" he said, and he 'cock-a-doodle-dooed' in his loudest voice.

The little mouse's mouth fell open in alarm and he panicked. "I must go," squeaked the mouse to the cat and with that, he scurried around a bale of hay and through a hole in the barn wall. The cat stopped purring and glared at the rooster. "You're always ruining my fun," she said coldly to the rooster.

When the little mouse finally found his way home, he told his mother what had happened. He told her of the terrible, scary monster he had seen and the lovely, silky cat that he had made friends with. His mother listened carefully. "You had a lucky escape, child," she said when he had finished.

"Yes, I'm glad that rooster didn't eat me," said the little mouse.

"No," replied his mother. "The rooster wouldn't have harmed you. I was talking about the cat. That soft, friendly creature wanted to eat us both for dinner. The rooster arrived just in time to save you."

The little mouse was very sorry to have misjudged the rooster and was careful never to trust the wrong person again.

Appearances are not always what they seem.

The Crow
- and the -
Pitcher

There once was a clever crow who was cunning and wise in everything he did. Crow could crack open a nut just by flying high in the air and dropping it onto some hard stones. He didn't even need to use his beak. Crow would never go hungry like the other birds and could always find tasty treats for dinner. Simply by doing a little dance on the soil, Crow could make the worms pop up to see what was going on.

The clever bird had a very good brain indeed and he knew how to use it. Then one day, Crow needed to be cleverer than he had ever been before.

It was a hot, dry, summer's day and Crow had been having a lovely time flying around. By the afternoon, he became very thirsty and all he wanted was a cool drink of water. Crow flew over hills and fields looking for a pond or a stream to drink from, but he couldn't find one anywhere. Soon, Crow was nearly ready to give up. "I don't know where else to look," he said, with a very dry throat. "There isn't a drop of water to be found anywhere."

Just then, Crow saw a cottage far below him and flying closer, he suddenly spotted a table in the garden. In the middle of the table was a tall, glass pitcher of water. By now, Crow was even more thirsty, so he swooped down to take a closer look.

When Crow flew down to the table and tried to stick his head into the neck of the pitcher, he found that it was much too narrow for him to take a drink from. He almost got his head stuck.

Still desperate for a drink, Crow perched on the table and stared at the pitcher. He could see that the pitcher was only half full of water, and it would need to be full all the way to the top so that Crow could easily dip his beak in to take a drink.

The Crow and the Pitcher

Crow hopped around the table with his head cocked on one side, thinking hard for a way to reach the water. Then, Crow noticed that the path leading up to the cottage was covered with tiny, round pebbles. This gave him an idea.

Crow hopped off the table where the pitcher stood and picked up one of the pebbles. Flying back to the table, he dropped the pebble into the pitcher. It fell to the bottom with a PLOP! Then, he went back for another pebble and another, plopping them into the water each time.

Each time Crow dropped a pebble into the water, it took up space. The more pebbles that Crow dropped in, the more space they took up. Soon, the water began to be pushed up to the top, until the pitcher was nearly full enough for Crow to take a sip.

"It's working!" he squawked, hopping up and down and flapping his wings with excitement. "I'll soon be able to drink," Crow said. He worked all evening filling the pitcher with pebbles and eventually, Crow's task was done.

"This is the moment I've been waiting for," Crow said, and he put his beak into the neck of the pitcher where he could finally reach the water. He drank and drank and drank until he could drink no more. Finally, he lifted up his head and gave a great, "CAW" of relief.

"Problems can always be solved by looking around and making the best of what you've got," said the wise crow as he took flight once more. He flew back home fully refreshed, delighted with how clever he had been.

Where there's a will, there's a way.

The Lion
- and the -
Elephant

In the jungle, the lion was king. Splendid and magnificent, he would roam around knowing he had been chosen, out of all the other animals, to be King of the Beasts. Fearless and courageous, he ruled the animal world and everyone was in awe of him. Well, almost everyone. There was one animal who was not at all in awe of the lion and didn't care one bit whether he pleased him or not.

That animal was a rooster and he loved to crow all morning. His crowing was so loud that it would wake all of the other animals up and none hated his crowing more than the lion. In fact, for some reason even the lion himself did not understand, he even began to feel fearful of the time in the morning when the rooster would make his horrible noise.

On one particular morning, the sun came up and the rooster began to crow as usual. "COCK-A-DOODLE-DO!" he went. "COCK-A-DOODLE-DO!" The sound was so shrill and loud, it upset the lion. Sitting up, he put his paws over his ears.
"Go away!" the lion cried, "Go away!" The rooster had no intention of going away at all.
"COCK-A-DOODLE-DO!" he crowed, again. "Wake up! It's a beautiful day."

The lion groaned. "Why is it," he asked himself, "that I, the mighty King of the Beasts, am afraid of a harmless rooster? It ought to be the other way around. The rooster should be afraid of me!" With that, the lion let out a blood-curdling roar.

The rooster turned his head to one side and listened. "Pooh!" he said to himself. "If Mr. Big-and-Mighty Lion thinks he is going to scare me off like that, he's got another thing coming." Then, the sly rooster lifted his head, opened his beak wide, and cock-a-doodle-dooed even louder than the lion's roar.

The lion shuddered at the sound and felt ashamed of his fear. "Is it only me," he asked himself, "or are other animals afraid of silly things, too? I must find out."

So, he ventured out into the jungle to see what the other animals had to say.

First, he came across some monkeys swinging through the trees. "Monkeys," the lion called out, "are there any silly things you are afraid of?" The monkeys stopped swinging and looked thoughtful.

"We sometimes get scared of being eaten by lions like you!" they said.

"What about the crowing of the rooster?" asked the lion.

The monkeys started to giggle. "You must be joking," they laughed.

The lion skulked away in embarrassment, ending up by the river. There, he came across the hippopotamus. "You are big and strong, like me, Hippopotamus," called the lion. "Is there anything silly you are afraid of?" The hippopotamus stopped what he was doing and stared at the lion.

"I'm afraid of the crocodile's teeth," he said with a shiver. "They are pointy and sharp. I wouldn't like to be bitten by him!"

"What about the crowing of the rooster?" asked the lion. The hippopotamus blew a stream of bubbles out of his nose.

"You must be joking," he smirked.

Just then, an elephant came lumbering out of the jungle in a hurry. "The elephant is very wise," thought the lion, so he decided to ask him what he thought. Leaving the hippopotamus giggling behind him, he ran to catch up with the elephant. "Can I speak to you for a moment, Elephant?" he asked, politely.

"Not just now, Lion, I have a serious problem," the elephant replied, looking worried. Then, he shook his head so hard that the lion thought the elephant's ears would come off.

"I have a serious problem, too," the lion admitted. The elephant could see that the lion was distressed.

"If you tell me your problem," Elephant said, "then I'll tell you mine." So, the lion lowered his voice, ashamed to say the words.

"Every morning when I hear the rooster crow, I feel afraid," he whispered.

"I know how you feel, Lion," said the elephant. "My fear is that if a mosquito flies into my ear, I will die!" The elephant gave his head another massive shake.

"How silly that the mighty elephant is afraid of such a small thing as a mosquito," the lion thought to himself. Then he realized how silly his own fear was.

"Thank you, Elephant," said the lion, brightly. "Now that I know I am not the only one with silly fears, I feel much better." The elephant thought about this for a minute and began to chuckle. The lion joined in and soon, the roar of their laughter was heard all around the jungle.

Now, when the rooster crows in the morning, the lion is no longer afraid. "It's only a sound," he tells himself. "It cannot hurt me." When the elephant hears the buzzing of the mosquito, he tells himself exactly the same thing.

Everyone has something they are afraid of.

The Hare
- and the -
Hound

There once was a farmer who led a very busy life on his farm. There were animals to look after, crops to grow, hay to be harvested, and apples and plums to be picked. The farmer worked very hard, but he enjoyed it because he had a faithful hound who was his helper.

The hound had big, bright eyes and soft, shiny fur. He loved protecting the farm and helping his master. The hound's job was to chase away any animals that tried to eat the crops, which the farmer had worked so hard to grow.

One lovely summer's day, the farmer and the hound were out walking in the fields when the farmer saw a hare eating his crop of juicy carrots. "Chase that greedy hare away from my carrots!" shouted the farmer to his hound.

The hound bounded forward, ready for a game of chase. The hare saw him and immediately turned to flee, as the hound darted after her with a joyful bark. "Make sure she doesn't come back," the farmer called after the hound. "If you catch her, you can have her for dinner," he added.

Like a streak of lightning, the hound raced across the meadow after the hare. They ran over hills and valleys, through woods and across streams. The hare was just in front and the hound just a few lengths behind. Neither slowed for an instant.

Mile after mile they ran. The hare was determined to get away and the hound was determined to catch her. "This is the best game of chase I've ever had," the hound thought to himself. He was having a great time, but the hare certainly wasn't. She didn't think it was a game at all. The hare was running for her life!

After a while, the hare glanced behind her. The hound seemed to be getting closer. "I will have to try and outwit the hound, if I'm going to escape him," panted the hare.

Without any warning, the hare made a sharp turn and darted left. Then, she made another turn and darted right. She zigzagged backwards and forwards. Then, suddenly, she turned and ran towards the hound, jumped over his head and ran off in the opposite direction.

The hound felt like laughing. "The hare is a great runner," he said, grinning, "but she won't get away from me that easily."

At last, the hare was getting tired and she started to slow down. "I can catch her now, if I want to," the hound panted. The hare could feel the heat of the hound's breath on her back and feeling very scared, she glanced behind her.

When the hound saw the terrified look on the hare's face, he suddenly felt sorry for her. "I don't really want to catch her," he thought, slowing down. "It's been a great chase, but I didn't want to scare her that much. I just wanted to teach her a lesson not to go after my master's carrots."

With that, the hound slowed down and allowed the hare to get away. She quickly escaped down a burrow, heading home to her three little baby hares.

When the hound arrived back at the farm, his master was waiting. When he saw that the hound hadn't caught the hare, he gave a chuckle. "Was the hare too fast for you?" asked the farmer, patting the hound on the head. "I never thought I'd see the day you were outrun by a little pest like that."

The hound just smiled and flopped down in his bed, tired and happy. "I'm glad I let the hare go in the end," he thought to himself. "It's one thing to run for your dinner, but quite another to run for your life!"

Winning often depends on who needs to win the most.

The Fox
- and the -
Crow

Once, there was a large, black crow that had made her nest, high in a tree. The crow had a proud head, bright eyes, glossy black feathers and a strong beak. One day, she brought a large piece of yellow cheese back to her nest and held it in her beak.

The crow waved the cheese around so that the wonderful smell wafted around her. "I won't eat it straight away," thought the crow. "I shall hold it in my beak for a while and think about how good it is going to taste. Then, when I do eat it, it will taste even more delicious."

Watching the crow from his den in the woods was a cunning fox and he was very hungry. Even from a distance, the fox could smell the cheese and it made his mouth water. He wanted that cheese for himself. "If I can't talk a mere crow into letting me have that piece of cheese," he said to himself, "then my name is not Fox!"

When the fox reached the tree where the crow sat, he called to her, "Beautiful Crow, that piece of cheese is far too large for one bird. Wouldn't you like to share it with a poor, hungry creature like myself?"

"I went to a lot of trouble to find this cheese," the crow thought to herself. "Why should I share it with anyone? If the fox has half, then there will be less for me and I'm hungry."

The fox could tell from the look in the crow's eyes that she wasn't convinced, so he tried again. "Lovely Crow," he said, using nearly all of his charm, "if you eat that cheese all at once, it will make you plump and round and you're so lovely the way you are." The crow could see a gleam in the fox's eyes.

"He'll say anything to get my cheese," she thought to herself. "I'll just ignore him." So, the wily fox tried a different approach.

"Exquisite Crow, how can we talk properly when you are so far away? I'd climb the tree and join you if I could, but foxes can't climb very high. Why don't you fly down and join me, then we can discuss the matter between us, as friends?"

"Aha!" thought the crow, turning her back on the fox. "If he thinks I'm going to fall for that old trick, he's wrong. The minute I join him on the ground, he'll eat my cheese."

Next, the fox tried to flatter the crow by showering her with praise. "Glorious Crow," he said in his smoothest, silkiest voice, "I've been told you have the most beautiful singing voice." The crow was pleased with this compliment, but said nothing.

"In fact," the fox went on, "I've been told that you can sing more sweetly than nightingales, who are famous for their beautiful song." The crow preened her feathers a little. She was very pleased by the fox's kind words.

The fox realized his flattery was beginning to work on the crow, so he went on, "I've even heard that when the song-thrush hears you sing, he wishes that he could reach the high notes as sweetly."

This was too much for the foolish crow. She just had to impress the fox with her voice. The crow flung back her head and opened her beak as wide as she could. "CAW!" she sang loudly. "CAW!"

"Aha!" cried the fox, gleefully, as the large piece of tasty, yellow cheese fell from the crow's beak and straight into the fox's open mouth.

Careful not to let go of the cheese, the fox mumbled, "You should never fall for flattery, Crow. It is most unwise to believe everything people say to you."

"I may be easily flattered," said the crow, "but you are a trickster! You will go to any lengths to get what you want."

"That's just the way I am, Crow," said the fox, pleased with how he had outsmarted her.

"No hard feelings?" With that, the disappointed crow watched the fox scamper away with the cheese she had been looking forward to eating herself.

The fox didn't stop until he had reached his den. Once he was safe inside, he placed the cheese carefully on a plate in front of him and licked his lips. He tied a napkin around his neck and settled down to the meal he had worked so hard to win. "At last! I can't wait to eat my tasty cheese," he thought. "I will dine like a king tonight!" The fox ate up every last delicious morsel and it was all thanks to the crow's foolish vanity.

Always beware of flattery.

The Bundle
- of -
Sticks

There once was a carpenter who had four sons. They always did whatever their father asked of them, but were always arguing because they were all so different. "I love working outside," proclaimed the strong, athletic son.

"I'd rather eat my breakfast," said the plump son.

The lazy son yawned and said, "I prefer to read a book."

"I don't have time for any of that," said the handsome son, holding up a mirror. "I need to comb my hair."

The carpenter worried about his sons arguing. "If they can't work together now, how will they manage when I am no longer here?" he thought to himself. He called his sons to him and said, "I am getting old and I'm sad to see that you can't get along. Why can't you stop quarreling and work together?" The boys were silent. Their arguing had become a habit.

The carpenter rocked backwards and forwards in his chair on the porch, trying to come up with a solution. Then, he had a bright idea. "I want you to go into the woods and bring me back one small stick, each," he said. "They must be about this long," he continued, holding his hands a little ways apart.

The sons were puzzled by this request, but they loved their father, so they did as they were told. One by one, they entered the woods in search of a stick.

It didn't take long for the four sons to find four sticks, but the ones they each chose were very different. "My stick is strong and resilient," said the athletic son.

"Mine is beautiful," said the handsome son. "It must be the finest stick in the woods."

"Mine is nice and round, like me," said the plump son.

"I don't care what mine is like," said the lazy son, "as long as it's easy to carry home."

When the sons returned home, the old man tied their four sticks into a bundle. "I challenge you to break this over your knee," he said, handing the bundle to the strongest son. "A little bundle like that?" scoffed the son. "Easy!" He put the bundle over his knee and strained with all his might, but he couldn't break it. Then, his three brothers tried. The plump brother jumped up and down on it. The vain brother stood on a chair and dropped it. The lazy son threw it at the wall, but the bundle remained unbroken.

The carpenter separated the bundle and gave the sticks back to his sons. "Now, try the same thing with just one stick," he said.

This time, the sticks broke easily. The boys were amazed that when the four sticks were tied together, they were impossible to break, but apart they snapped like twigs. "You are like these four sticks," the wise old carpenter said to his sons. "The four of you are strong together, but on your own you are weak. If you work together as a team, you will be able to achieve anything you want."

The four brothers soon learned the lesson their father had taught them. Even though they were all very different, they agreed they would work together and stop quarreling over petty things. They lost the habit of arguing over nothing and instead, they became friends, as brothers should be.

The sons were grateful to their father and would often sit with him on the porch, at the end of the day. It made the carpenter very happy to hear how strong his sons were when they worked together, just as the bundle of sticks could not be broken when they were tied together.

United you will stand, but divided you may fall.